KLASKY CSUPO INC.

Based on the TV series *Rugrats*® created by Arlene Klasky, Gabor Csupo, and
Paul Germain as seen on Nickelodeon®

SIMON SPOTLIGHT
An imprint of Simon & Schuster Children's Publishing Division
1230 Avenue of the Americas,
New York, New York 10020

Manufactured in the United States of America
First Edition
2 4 6 8 10 9 7 5 3 1
ISBN 0-689-82854-3
Library of Congress Catalog Card Number 99-71390

A Rugrats Night Before Christmas

by David Lewman
illustrated by Sergio Cuan

Simon Spotlight/Nickelodeon

'Twas the night afore Christmas—our house was real still.
Not a baby was cryin'—nope, not even Dil.

Our stockings were hung by the chimbly in pairs,
So Santa could fill them with sweet Dummi bears.

We babies were trying to sleep in our beds,
But pictures of Reptar bars danced in our heads.

I was wearing warm jammies, all fuzzy and new;
So were Chuckie, Phil, Lil, and Angelica, too.

I'd started to dream about shiny new toys,
When outside I heard a strange jingly noise!
Then Lil said, "Did you hear an elf or a fairy?"
And Chuckie said, "No, I heard something real scary!"

I pulled out my studriver—Phil said, "Yeah, try it!"
Angelica yawned, "You dumb babies, be quiet!"

I flipped back the hook and climbed out of my crib,
Then crawled to the window and sawed—it's no fib—
Some kind of a wagon that looked like our sleds
Being pulled by big doggies with sticks on their heads!

The doggies looked wild, but they must've been tame,
'Cause the man in the wagon-sled called 'em by name:

"Now, Dasher! Now, Dancer! Now, Prancer and Vixen!
On, Comet! On, Cupid! On, Donner and Blitzen!"

As soon as they heard him, without even tryin',
Those stick-headed doggies were floatin' and flyin'!
They flied way, way up to the top of our roof,
And when Spike heard their feets go "click click," he said, "Woof!"

"Come on, Chuckie," I said, "let's see what made Spike bark."
"But, Tommy," he said, "I'm a-scared of the dark!"

We walked down the stairs (well, um, really we sneaked),
And what do you think that we sawed when we peeked?

In the chimbly we sawed two big boots hanging down.
"Look at those big shoes!" Chuckie cried. "It's a clown!"

"It's Santa!" squeaked Lil, who had crawled down behind us.
Then Phil whispered, "What'll we do if he finds us?"

"We gots to be quiet," I whispered right back.
"Let's see if he eats all his good nummy snack."
My mom said the treats were for "when Santa comes,"
But Angelica found them and left mostly crumbs.

Then Lil said, "At least he'll have something that squirms—
We left him a couple of really nice worms!"

But Phil said, "We ate all those worms—me and you."
And Lil said, "Did not, Philip!" Phil said, "Did too!"

Whatever was left Santa ate for his snack.
Then he drank the warm cocoa and opened his sack.

I was counting the presents—"One, six, two, three, nine . . ."
When Angelica shouted, "Those toys are all MINE!"

She had creeped up behind us right there on the stair.
"Oh, no," I was thinking, "that wouldn't be fair!"

Then Santa looked over and just shook his head.
Angelica sat down and quietly said,
"I mean, they're for everyone—not just for me."
Santa smiled and put more presents under the tree.

Then I heard Santa 'sclaim as he flew out of sight,
"Merry Christmas to all, and to all, nighty-night!"